ROOM FOR ONE MORE.

written by
SANDY BARTON

illustrated by
MARK LEISER

In memory of Gloria, giver of cookies and kindness.

xoxo

Sandy

For my two little ladies, and the Umbrella Man,

who introduced me to Sandy.

Mark

THINGS TO DO...

BEFORE YOU READ

Find a comfy place to read, get all snuggly.

Look at the cover. Gather as much information as you can before you start. Get your mind ready for the adventure!

Sometimes it's fun to read with a friend, sometimes it's nice to read alone.

WHILE YOU'RE READING

Make it interesting. Change voices for the different characters. Read parts or the whole thing out loud.

Make a movie in your head as you read. Turn the words into pictures and make them come alive!

Take a few minutes every so often to make predictions. What do you think might happen next?

Remember, predictions are not right or wrong, they just happen or they don't!

WHEN YOU FINISH THE BOOK

Tell a friend or someone in your family about the story - but don't spill the beans, just give them a short summary.

Think about your favorite parts, or your not so favorite parts. What were they and why?

Write a book of your own. Now that's a GREAT adventure!

CONTENTS

ROOM FOR ONE MORE

I REMEMBER WHEN

Being the "big" friend of a leprechaun has been, well, interesting to say the least. I've lived through the hilarious experience of first discovering my good friend, Mr. McAllister, a funny little leprechaun with a very big heart. I've lived through meeting his entire village in my back woods and having my ankles hugged by all of them. I've even lived through moving him and all 160 of his relatives and friends from our old woods to our new woods!

It sure was a wild, wacky, wickedly funny crosstown adventure in my van – with 161 of my new closest friends. I've lived through... oh honestly, there are far too many happy memories of things we've done to list them here, so you'll have to trust me. My days as a leprechaun's friend are never dull.

For those of you who haven't heard the story, after my family was all moved into our new house, and the leprechauns were all settled in their new homes in the woods, life began to feel normal again. I guess normal isn't really a good word to describe life with leprechauns. Maybe a better word would be magical, since so many days were filled with their delightful tricks and clever ideas. Chilly winter days brought the Leprechaun Olympics, and more laughing and cheering than I've ever done in my life. Spring days meant repairs, lots of building and St. Patrick's Day, of course. During the lazy days of summer you could always find those wee folks down in the creek, splashing each other or floating around on their rafts. I love all of the memories we've piled up together!

When my family had to move yet again, we were sad thinking that we would have to leave our dear little friends, but we knew it was not the end of our friendship. I promised Mr. McAllister that I'd visit often, a promise we sealed with a pinky swear.

As you know, when you wrap your pinky finger around someone else's pinky finger, that's your word and you have to keep it. So as I walked away from him on that last day, I blew a kiss in his direction. I'm not sure if he knew that I saw him catch it and stuff it into his pocket. That made me happy; I hope it made him happy, too. I think that's what friendship is supposed to feel like.

ELEVEN YEARS AGO

WHAT'S YOUR PROBLEM?

On the day I drove away from that old house I had lots of questions. Would we like living in the city? How would it feel not having a huge woods behind our house? Would Rosie, the mourning dove that delivers Mr. McAllister's messages to me, be able to find us? Would the new owners notice if I crept back along the path to the leprechauns' village? Would I be able to keep their homes a secret?

Oh, my mind was so tired from worrying! I figured I would know the answers soon enough, and that all the worrying in the world wasn't going to change anything. Besides, leprechauns don't believe in worrying. Whenever I had a problem,

Mr. McAllister always said, "No worries. Stay calm. Think about what kind of a problem you have, then make a plan."

I wasn't sure what he meant by "what kind of a problem". I always thought a problem was a problem, so I asked him one day. What he told me was really quite helpful. He suggested that when I have a problem I must decide if it's something I can handle myself, if it's something I need to ask for help with, or if it's something I can't do anything about. He also warned that being afraid and freaking out doesn't solve any problem. I thought it was pretty good advice. (Besides, Mr. McAllister told me a very, very surprising thing, but sh-hhhhhhhh, please don't let on that you know this. He told me that when leprechauns are afraid, and it sometimes happens but not very often, their magical powers get weak. Hmm, I wonder if that's true for us, too? Do we use up all of our energy by being afraid of things?)

I put my worries aside, and instead began learning all about our new neighborhood. There were stores nearby, there were neighbors - very close but very nice - and there were even a few sugar maple trees on our street! I couldn't wait till fall to see their leaves painted orange and red! I wondered if I could tap one of the bigger trees; after watching Mr. McAllister do it so many times in our woods, I thought I just might be able to do it myself. If it all went as I hoped, I could turn the sap into the most delicious maple syrup ever. From sap, to syrup, to pancakes, perfect! Yes, this new house was going to be just fine.

I looked out of the window on the fourth day at our new house and who do you think I saw? No, not Mr. McAllister, but Rosie the mourning dove! She was walking in circles in the backyard, making her sweet little cooing noise that I loved. I nearly fell flat on my face trying to get down the stairs and out the door that morning. Rosie walked over to me, anxious to get the message off from around her neck.

Her tan feathers were so soft, and her black eyes stared at me while I carefully untied the string that held the paper.

"Wait here Rosie," I whispered, and ran back into the house to get a pen and a handful of her favorite seeds. While she pecked contentedly at her treat, I sat in the grass and read Mr. McAllister's message.

I must admit, I was so excited to hear from him that my hands were shaking!

Dear Big One, (That's his nickname for me)

I'm missing you. Any chance of you stopping over sometime? We're having a problem with the new owner of the house and may need your help. She has a BIG dog. I don't want to go through THAT again. Remember how the Big Red Horse (that's my dog, Sophie), nearly scared the pants off of me when we first met?????

Oh, and Big One – GOOD NEWS! I've fixed the raft and have made lots of donuts.

Your friend,
Mr. CW McAllister

I quickly wrote my reply on the paper:

Dear Mr. McAllister,

I am so happy to hear from you,

but just a little worried about your problem.

You always say not to worry, so I'll try not to.

We'll stay calm and think this through – together.

I'm glad that you asked for help;

this does sound like a job for two.

I'm missing you, too! Good for you – you fixed the rafts, and

now you're making donuts? When did you learn how to do

that? I'm going to gobble up a few when I come over!

See you tomorrow morning.

Wait for me at the meeting circle.

Bye for now,

Sandy

Rosie stood very still while I rolled up the paper
and tied it to the string around her neck. She fluttered
onto my arm, cooed her good-bye and flew away.

SLIP SLIDING away

The next morning I grabbed my sketch pad, a pencil and a handful of grapes from the refrigerator. Mr. McAllister loves to make grape juice so I try to remember to take him grapes when I can. The sketch pad came in handy when I had to disguise my real reason for going back into the woods at my old house. If the neighbors asked what I was doing, I had to make up something. I couldn't exactly say, "Oh, I'm just going back to visit my leprechaun friends." They'd think I was crazy! Besides, I really do love to draw the trees back there, so it's a believable story I think.

Miss Gloria, the next door neighbor, and the sweetest woman in the world, was out in her garden when I drove up.

"Hi Miss Gloria! How are you doing? I see your day lilies are blooming and beautiful!"

She waved her hello. "Sandy wait here," she said, and scurried into the house. In no time flat she was back out with a plate of cookies, still warm from the oven.

"Miss Gloria, you make the best cookies, thank you!"

"Take more, take more, and take some home for the family," she insisted. I did NOT refuse. Miss Gloria's cookies were the best, and you'd have to have gumballs in your head to say no.

"What are you doing? Are you going back to draw more trees?"

"Yep, you know me, Miss Gloria. I always come prepared in case I see a beautiful tree I just have to sketch. Besides, I really miss the woods. Do you mind if I go back through your yard?"

"Of course I don't mind dear. You go back and have a nice walk. Knock on my window when you leave so I can say good-bye."

The path through her yard was wet with dew and my toes felt cold by the time I got to the meeting circle. I looked around but saw no one. Then a pine cone dropped at my feet. I looked around again. "Mr. McAllister? Are you here?" I whispered. Another pine cone dropped, this time on my head. Now I KNEW he was near. I looked up and sure enough, there he was on the branch above me, jumping up and down, making a pine needle shower.

"Big One! I'm not playing me tricks, I'm jumping 'cause I'm just so happy to see you!" And in a blink he was standing at my feet, hugging my ankles with all his might.

"I'm happy to see you, too, you silly leprechaun. Now come here and sit down. Tell me what's going on. You said you have a problem. I'll help if I can."

"Oh Big One, the BIG problem is a BIG dog. Your big red horse of a dog, Sophie, was big, but she was nothing but an overgrown smoosh. She was curious and stuck her nose into my house that one time, but she was never mean, don't ya know. This BIG dog is mean. And it has the strangest slime coming out of its mouth all the time."

I couldn't help but chuckle picturing a huge, drooling dog chasing Mr. McAllister. All the magic in the world won't work against a drooling dog that's about to slime you! "Mr. McAllister, the slime is drool. All dogs, especially big dogs, drool – a lot! If you get slimed it won't hurt you, it will just be kind of disgusting for a while."

"Well don't ya be smilin', Big One. I can see ya think this is one funny joke, but it isn't. One day he ran after me so fast, I was screamin' like a baby. Screamin' I tell you, and I'm not proud of it! He had his mouth open ready to eat me for sure, and just as he was about to chomp down on me, a gust of wind whirled through the trees, took that mouthful of slime, and blew it all over me. I kept right on screamin', but I must have had me some Irish luck because by then I was right in front of my door. A slippery mess I was and I slid right through it and landed in a heap in front of the fireplace. I was covered in slime, doncha know! That big, mean monster of a dog didn't know where I disappeared to! As sure as I'm sittin' here today, he would have had me for dinner if the wind hadn't picked me up off my feet."

"Mr. McAllister, mean dogs are a serious problem. Getting slimed is not. Let's think about it and come up with a plan to keep you safe from that giant drool machine."

SCREAMING SKUNKS

I spent most of the morning visiting with my wee friends and checking out how the rafts had been mended. I must admit, I was just a little disappointed to find out that the donuts were not quite what I thought they'd be. In fact, they weren't food at all! Instead, these donuts were circles of wood used for floating in the creek. After he stopped laughing at my disappointment, Mr. McAllister described how he made them, and as usual, it was very clever!

First he cut down a small tree and sawed it into slices. He took one wooden slice and traced a smaller circle in the center of it. Once there was an outline of the circle, he drilled holes all around the outline... kind of like a dotted line. Then it got really fun.

Balancing one of the slices between two stumps, he had his friend jump from a tree onto the center of the slice and poof! The center popped out and left the outside circle looking just like a wooden donut! The leprechaun kids were floating down the creek on their new donuts that day, and it looked like so much fun!

By the end of the morning we had decided on a plan to keep the mean dog out of the woods. I would go talk with the owner before I left and tell her a true story that might make her think twice about letting her dog run loose in the woods. On my way down the path, I sketched a quick drawing of a white birch tree just so my "excuse" would be true, and I said my goodbyes to Mr. McAllister. I could tell he felt much better knowing that his problem would soon be solved. Sitting around chatting with my old friend was a really good way to spend the morning; it was just like old times, and I knew it would always feel that way. Cutting across the backyards I could see Miss

Gloria picking some apples from her tree. She had a bag of cookies all ready for me, along with a nice hug.

"Thanks again for the yummy treats. I'll see you soon," I promised. "You know how I like to sketch trees!" Oh how I wished I could tell her about the leprechauns. She would love meeting them and I was sure she would have kept the secret, but I also had to keep my promise and not tell anyone about them.

The new owner was coming out just as I was about to knock on her door. "Hi!" I said. " I stopped by to see Miss Gloria and do some sketching in the back, and it occurred to me that I forgot to warn you about the woods. Your dog might run into a little problem back there if he gets loose. He's likely to run into a stinky skunk. My dog did and she got sprayed more than once. She stunk to high heaven! So you might want to keep your dog closer to the house or even in the front yard. Luckily the yard is huge, so he'll still have plenty of room to run around."

"Skunks? Skunks? Oh I can't have him getting

sprayed by a skunk!" she screamed. " We'll have to put clothespins on our noses for a month! Thank you so much for telling me. I'll be sure to keep my sweet little Pookie out of the woods." She stopped for a minute then said, " Hmmmm. Come to think of it, one day he was back there and was chasing something. He was barking and growling and for some reason, I thought I heard screaming. But, skunks don't scream ... do they?"

I tried to be very serious and answered, "Uh, no, I don't think so. They usually snort and hit their paws on the ground before they spray, kind of like a final warning. But scream, no, they don't scream."

It was so hard not to laugh. Skunks screaming - ha! If she only knew that the screaming was coming from my little leprechaun friend, just before he got slimed by her dog!

She continued. "Well I was sure I heard screaming. I ran back there with a leash and brought him home. I bet it was the skunk he was chasing!

Maybe they make a screaming sound. I'm thinking of putting a fence around the yard anyway, so this might be another reason to do that. I don't even go back in the woods at all. There's nothing worth seeing back there. Aren't you afraid you'll run into a skunk?"

"No," I said, trying not to smile, "I just sit in one spot and draw. I've never had a problem."

"Well, feel free to go through my yard anytime you want. You don't have to ask, and thank you again for the warning. My dog and I will stay stink-free!" As she walked back into the house I could hear her mumbling, "I'm sure I heard screaming. It must have been the skunk. Screaming skunks - what next!"

I turned around and could see Mr. McAllister standing on a branch of a very tall pine tree (using a little bit 'o magic to get up there I suppose), giving me a thumbs up and a wink. Problem solved. I gave him a wave and a wink, took my bag of cookies, and headed home.

a NEW PLAN

Being at the old house again made me realize how important friends are. Good friends. The kind of friends who trust you enough to share problems and ask for help, the kind of friends who you can do absolutely nothing with and still have fun, the kind of friends you'll do anything for, any time – any place. Miss Gloria and Mr. McAllister are friends like that; because of them, I felt happy all day.

That's what led me to my next plan. More than anything, I wanted these two special friends to meet each other. Making that happen would not be an easy task. Miss Gloria would probably think I was crazy, but would think it was funny, anyway. I had a big job ahead of me if I was going to convince her that leprechauns are real, and there were 161 of them living about 300 feet from her back door. If I could make her believe those two things, I knew she'd be the best friend a leprechaun could hope for.

As for Mr. McAllister, he had already seen Miss Gloria from a distance, but it would take some fancy talking to get him to agree to let her in on our secret. It wasn't impossible, but it was going to be like putting snowflakes back into the clouds. So, I had to come up with some pretty good reasons why I wanted them to meet. Leprechauns are very logical little creatures. If something seems to make perfect sense, then, it's ok. If there's no sense in it – forget about it! What would YOU say to Miss Gloria and Mr. McAllister to convince them that they should meet?

I'LL BE HAPPY TO SHARE

Because I really wanted this plan to work, I took my time thinking about it. This was a problem I could take care of myself, so I took out my sketchbook and wrote down my ideas one by one. By the end of a week, I had enough reasons, I thought, and decided to take a drive over to the old house to talk with each of them. I'd start with Mr. McAllister.

Monday was a beautiful summer day and I think the birds agreed. They were singing in the trees when I pulled into Miss Gloria's driveway. Of course there were about 23 different songs being sung, so it was like listening to a whole bunch of radio stations at once! A little confusing and hard to sing along, but a beautiful mess of music in its own little way!

I found my wee friend hammering nails into a NO TRESPASSING sign. Of course it was so small no big person would ever see it, but I had a feeling it was meant for a four legged beast named 'The Mean Dog', or should I say, 'Pookie'!

"Big One, I didn't expect to see you today! Were ya missin' your favorite Irishman?"

"Of course I miss you, but I have something important to talk with you about. Do you have a minute to sit?"

We found a spot near the pond that was thick with grass and smelled like summertime. There were chubby frogs croaking on the mossy logs, and dragon flies were practicing taking off and landing on a nearby rock. I didn't quite know how to begin, so I just started talking.

"Mr. McAllister, now that I'm not living here anymore, I'm a little worried about you and the folks in the village. What if you run into trouble and need help fast? I can't get here as quickly as I used to. What if you run out of food? What if you need supplies that you can't find here? What if..."

Before I could finish my sentence he interrupted, "Have ya forgotten what I told ya a long time ago about worryin'? It will do nothing but give ya a belly ache, Big One. Besides, you're the only big person who knows about us, so there IS no one else to take your place. Don't ya be worrying about us, we'll be fine."

"What if I could promise you that there's another person who could be trusted to know the secret. What if that person lived very close and was just about the nicest, kindest person in the whole world. What would you think of that? And what if that person lived alone and just might love to have a new friend. Would you be willing to meet her?"

There was a long silence. Very long. I patiently waited for his answer. I looked at him as he twitched his nose, scratched his head, closed his eyes and stroked his beard – then did it all over again.

Oh, he was thinking hard about this one! Finally he cleared his throat. "Ahem. Big One, this is a complicated thing you're suggestin'. I believe you wouldn't be askin' me to do this unless you were very sure it was ok. But, honestly... I don't like the idea of anyone knowing about us. On the other hand me dear friend, surely I understand why you are concerned. Look at what happened with The Mean Dog. You saved me from a lifetime of slime attacks. I needed your help. My magic was fading because I was afraid, and I thank me lucky stars that I was close to home. Hmmm." More silence. "And ya say this woman lives alone, Big One? She's feelin' a bit of loneliness, is she?"

"Mr. McAllister, yes, she lives alone. Her husband passed away a few years ago and she misses him terribly, but she never ever complains. She's such a lovely woman AND she's a wonderful cook. There's a good chance she'd make you cookies, cakes, picnic lunches, almost anything you can think of. But most of all, she'd be a good friend to you, your family and your friends. I can promise you that much. The best way I can say it is – I'd like to share her with you, and you with her. My two dear friends being friends with each other! I think that would be fabulous, don't you?"

He started playing with his beard again and looked at me with a very serious stare. "Big One, this is a matter of trust, ya know. I have to really and truly believe you think it's a good idea. You need to pinky swear on this one. I'll be needin' your word, my dear."

I reached over and stuck out my pinky finger. He wrapped his around mine and I promised that Miss Gloria would be a trustworthy, kind, honest, lovely friend for ever and ever.

"Pinky swear?"

"Pinky swear!" I said. My heart was smiling out loud! "Now, I'm going to talk with her and try to make her understand that YOU would be a good friend. You can be grouchy, and sometimes downright goofy, but I think you'd be good for each other. Wish me luck."

"Luck? I've got plenty of luck! I'm a leprechaun – doncha be forgettin' that." He reached into his pocket and pulled out a handful of gold. Poof - there I was standing in a shower of sparkling gold dust, as if the stars from the sky had all come down to dance for me. I felt a weird tingling all over – maybe that's how magic feels! By the time I reached Miss Gloria's back yard, everything had returned to normal, and I was ready for the next part of my plan.

WHOOPEE!

I t didn't take long before the cookies were brought out, coffee was poured and we were chatting about our families. I couldn't wait to get to the GOOD stuff!

"Miss Gloria, did you ever see something that was so strange you couldn't believe your eyes?"

"Let's see. Uh huh, once I saw a hummingbird. It was so small and so beautiful, and so fast I couldn't believe my eyes. So I guess I'd say yes. Why do you ask, dear?"

"Well, I um, gee I, um... funny you should mention something so small as a hummingbird. I saw something very small, too. Something so amazing that it took me a while before I believed I actually DID see it, I mean - him, um - them."

"Now you're confusing me, Sandy. 'It, him, them,' what do you mean?"

I decided to just spit it out. "I saw a leprechaun, Miss Gloria."

Miss Gloria took a bite of her cookie, a sip of her coffee, and all the while she looked over the top of her glasses at me. It seemed like a long time before she said anything. "A leprechaun. You saw a leprechaun. And did you slide down a rainbow together? Did you land in his pot of gold? Did he turn you into a pot belly pig and change you back again? Oh Sandy, you make me laugh with your jokes!"

"Miss Gloria, I'm not kidding," I said, taking her hands in mine. And looking her straight in the eyes I continued, "I. Met. A. Leprechaun. He is my dear friend. His name is Mr. McAllister and he lives right back there." She let her eyes follow my finger which was pointed at the woods, and her expression changed quite a bit. Her eyes opened wide, her mouth dropped open and made a perfect O.

"You're serious?"

"I'm serious."

"Back there?"

"Back there."

"In the woods?"

"In the woods."

Again there was a long pause. What came next made me fall off of my chair. She literally scared me out of my seat!

"Whoopee!" (Such an enormous noise coming from such a little lady like Miss Gloria!) "Can I meet him? Oh, you said them... are there more?"

"Oh yes. There are more. 160 more."

"WHAT? And they're all back there?"

"Yep."

Miss Gloria was jumping up and down, screaming with delight, clapping her hands. I sat there stunned. This was much easier than I thought it would be! She actually wanted to meet him, them!

So I began to tell her my tale. I told her about the

first time I met Mr. McAllister, how Sophie stuck her nose into his home under the tree. I told her about our meetings, the visit to school, the move across town in my van, the Leprechaun Olympics, and our sad "So long for a while" good-bye when I moved. She couldn't believe all that had happened right under her nose without ever knowing it! I wasn't allowed to leave until I told her as many things as I could remember about these little friends, and by the time I had run out of stories, or out of breath (I'm not sure what happened first), it was settled. Dear Miss Gloria promised to be a trusted friend to my wee friend, Mr. McAllister, and did her first ever pinky swear - then it was official. My friends were going to be friends.

"Well, when can I meet him? When, when?"

"How about Saturday," I said. "Noon?"

"Perfect!" she shouted. Putting her hands on her hips, she kicked up her legs in a little Irish jig, and danced her way down the hall. "I'm going to meet a leprechaun! I'm going to meet a leprechaun!"

I let myself out the back door and ran to the path in the woods. "Mr. McAllister! It's all set. You'll meet your new BIG friend on Saturday. See you at noon. Don't be late!" This time I jumped into the air and clicked my heels. I was so happy; it was like walking on clouds! Yippee!

a VISION OF GREEN

Friday night I had a hard time sleeping. I tossed and turned and kept wondering how the meeting would go. Would Mr. McAllister drop pine cones on poor Miss Gloria's head? Would he do something to scare her and send her screaming with fright through the woods? Would she think it was strange if lots of them came out and started hugging her ankles? Oh dear. I finally decided that everything would be fine, and next thing I knew, it was morning.

I jumped out of bed, made pancakes for the kids, and told my husband where I was going. He thought it was a great idea and wished me luck.

There was hardly any traffic so I pulled into Miss Gloria's driveway in record time.

I was a little nervous. You know how it feels when you do something for the first time... you're half excited and half scared? That's exactly how I felt. Gloria met me at the car.

"Sandy! I'm all ready!"

I couldn't believe my eyes. She was a vision of green. Every single thing she had on was green. I didn't know whether to laugh, scream, or pretend I didn't notice. Starting at ground level: green rain boots with big green frogs on the toes, green and white striped knee socks peeking out over the top of the boots, green and white plaid shorts with enormous pockets that came down to her knees, a green hoodie with the words: Everybody's Irish on St. Patrick's Day, a shamrock painted on her face and a tiny green bow in her hair. As I said, she was a vision of green.

"Miss Gloria, you're so... green!" I didn't know how else to say it. She was green from head to toe.

"Well, I AM meeting a leprechaun today, so I

thought I'd better make him feel comfortable."

"Miss Gloria, even a leprechaun doesn't wear THAT much green! But, you look adorable and I'm sure he'll be flattered that you wanted to make him happy." We walked, no, we jogged to the woods. I could hardly keep up with this green flash ahead of me. I tugged at her hood just as we got near the path, to slow her down. "Shhhh. Now you have to walk carefully. Our footsteps make very loud echoes underground. We don't want them to think there's an earthquake! Follow me."

Twigs cracked under our feet and the dry pine needles crunched as we walked. I suspected that Mr. McAllister was watching from above and waiting for the perfect moment to announce his arrival with a pine cone attack, a flutter of branches, or something dramatic. We no sooner got in front of his house when sure enough, a shower of pine needles fell from the tree above us. Miss Gloria never flinched. She stood there looking up with the biggest smile on her face.

I was so proud of her!

"Did he do that?" she whispered.

"Yep," I replied. "I'm sure he'll appear shortly (Ha! What a great pun, I thought!).

And just as I predicted, in a sparkling flash, there he was at our feet. This time HE was the one looking up. I could tell he was ready for the big day. His usually messy hair was combed neatly to the side, his scruffy beard was trimmed, and his britches had a new patch where an old tear had been. Yes, he was ready to meet his new friend.

"Mr. McAllister, I'd like you to meet my friend, Miss Gloria. Miss Gloria, this is my friend Mr. CW McAllister."

"Doncha know, it's my sincere pleasure to meet you," he said, putting his right arm across his belly and bowing deeply. I thought that was just about the cutest thing I had ever seen! Miss Gloria must have thought so too, because she had a grin on her face that went from ear to ear.

"I'm very pleased to meet you, Mr. McAllister. I've heard so many nice things about you from Sandy," she said while reaching into the two enormous pockets. She pulled out two bags of chocolate chip cookies, both tied with a green ribbon, of course. "I made you some cookies, but I made them smaller than usual so you could share them with your family."

The cookies were indeed small – about the size of a penny, just right for a leprechaun. Each one had tiny mountains of melted chocolate, a few nuts and golden brown dough. Yummy! Mr. McAllister's eyes lit up when he saw the bags of treats. He looked at me, then at Miss Gloria, then back at me and he winked. He reached into HIS pocket and pulled out a tiny package wrapped in a golden oak leaf, tied with a morning glory vine, its purple flowers still wet with dew.

"I've been thinkin'," he began, "what kind of a friend would I be if I didn't have a gift for you, so here is something Sandy will recognize. She was my first friend from the big world and I gave her one of these. And now I have another friend. Miss Gloria, this one is for you."

Miss Gloria carefully untied the morning glory ribbon and opened the leaf. There inside was a leprechaun friendship necklace, the same as the one he made for me many years ago. Three gold rings connected together – one ring for the leprechaun world, one for the big world, and one to show that they are now joined in friendship. Another vine was attached to the end to form a necklace.

"Now, if you can find it in ya to get down here, I'll be happy to help ya put it on, doncha know!"

Miss Gloria got down on her knees; the dear soul was nearly camouflaged in the green woods with all the green she was wearing! I watched as Mr. McAllister tenderly put the necklace over her head. When he was done, the two just looked at each other; two new friends, promising to be loyal, kind companions. I must admit, I noticed a few tear drops on my shirt... I was so happy, it made me cry!

GETTING TO KNOW YOU

The rest of the afternoon was filled with tours of the woods, talks about exciting things to come, plans for digging a secret tunnel to Miss Gloria's house, cookie menus, and adding a new seat at the meeting circle. There was so much to do, so much to see, and so much to look forward to. My heart was full knowing that this had all worked out so beautifully!

It was nearly 3 o'clock when I headed back to my car. I left Mr. McAllister and Miss Gloria back in the woods; they were busy picking raspberries and laughing with each one they popped into their mouths. Their red-stained lips gave a hint that they had eaten more than they had saved.

Later that night Miss Gloria called to tell me about her day. She was talking so fast I could hardly get a word in. "...and then he showed me his house under the roots of a really big pine tree. It's so cozy under there! And then he did this poof thing and a seat appeared for me at the meeting circle. And then he showed me the day care den, the rafts and donuts, the earthball, and the bobsled for the Leprechaun Olympics. There was so much to see, and he kept disappearing and re-appearing somewhere else. And then he called all of his family and friends in the village to come meet me and guess what, Sandy? They hugged my ankles! Oh it was a little weird at first, but they're not that tall, you know! It was such a fun afternoon I didn't want to come back to the house, but I had company coming for dinner and I had to get ready. It was so hard not to tell anyone about my new friends, but I made a promise and I kept it. Oh, oh, right now I'm looking out the back window and I can see the pussywillow torches around the meeting circle, or could it be the fireflies, dear?"

Whew, this was my first chance to talk, so I told

Miss Gloria that since I couldn't see the woods from my house in the city, I wasn't able to tell if she was looking at torches or fireflies, but I assured her that they were probably gathered in the meeting circle, talking about how wonderful it was to meet her too.

Early the next morning my two friends started working on their first project together. They had decided to make life jackets for the whole village. Now that they had the rafts and donuts, and an underground tunnel to the creek, they were anxious to spend their days by the water. As you can imagine, making that many life jackets isn't an easy job, but they had everything they needed right in the woods. Milkweed pods made great floaties for the little kids, and cattails were the best things ever for making life jackets. Getting enough for everybody was tough, but with Miss Gloria's help, they had a stack of cattails two feet high and three feet long in no time!

I had seen Mr. McAllister wearing one of these life jackets before, and he looked like a firefighter with an air pack on his back. Two brown cattails had straps made from vines that were attached with pine tree sap. All they had to do was put the cattails on their backs, tie the straps around the front and tah-dah, a life jacket! So, they had quite a project ahead of them and were eager to finish it. The creek looked cool and refreshing on those hot, humid days of July, and the thought of jumping right in made them all the more eager to work.

Rosie the mourning dove stopped by my house later that week with a message tied around her neck. She was pecking at the window when I came downstairs. "Hey Rosie, what do you have for me today, pretty girl?" I carefully unrolled the paper and was happy to read what it said.

The creek is sparkling; it's pretty deep
Let's have a picnic Friday, this week.
We'll bring the rafts, and all the stuff
The life jackets are done; we have enough.

Hope you can come, Miss Gloria, too

We'll play at the park-there's lots to do!

A picnic at the park with a bunch of leprechauns, what a blast. I wondered what kind of mischief they'd get into there! Of course I'd join them, so I wrote back to Mr. McAllister:

Thanks so much; I'll be there

But don't drop pine cones in my hair!

I'll bring the kayak; there's room for a bunch

When we get to the park, we'll eat some lunch.

Rosie took off with the message, and I thought about how funny it would be with all of those leprechauns in the kayak. There was plenty of room, but if they were going to be bouncing all around, we were going to be in for a wild ride!

Then I wondered if ANYTHING could be crazier than the ride in my van on moving day, all those years ago.

ROW, ROW, ROW YOUR BOAT

On Friday morning I tied the kayak to the roof of the car, packed a variety of very small sandwiches, put in a turkey sub for me, added lots of fruit, and a few other snacks. I also grabbed my life jacket because I knew cattails probably wouldn't work for me in an emergency! Before long I was ready to go and was so excited to be spending the day with such good friends.

Miss Gloria was going to meet us at the dock where she kept her own rowboat. She called it "The Silver Bullet" because it was silver, of course, and she claimed it shot through the water like a bullet. All of the scrapes and dents along its sides reminded me that it had seen its share of collisions with docks, logs and other sturdy objects. And oh, how Miss Gloria liked to row that thing down the creek! She was a fearless sailor with her white sun hat and puffy purple life jacket that matched the purple oars. It makes me smile just thinking about it.

The tunnel that brought the leprechauns safely to the creek had finally been completed and it really was a brilliant idea. I thought it was interesting to hear that they convinced some of the moles in the woods to help. They are, after all, very good at digging tunnels! In exchange for their work, the moles were given free access to the woods behind the leprechaun homes, so everybody was happy with the deal.

The entrance to the tunnel was under the bushes by the garage. From there, the tunnel curved through the bushes, under the road, down the little hill on the other side of the street, and ended next to the wooden dock on the creek. Leprechauns could walk the entire way without ever being seen. Plus, it was much safer than having to cross the street. Mr. McAllister once told me that he only had a problem with the tunnel two times. The first time was in May when he was half way through it and ran into a woodchuck coming from the other direction. I guess they scared each other so much that they both let out a scream, turned around, and ran back to where they had started. The second time was not so pleasant, in fact it stunk! It really did! Mr. McAllister was in the tunnel, almost to the creek, when he ran smack into a skunk. It was so dark, he never saw it coming until it was too late. That's when he saw the white stripe rising up into the air and - psssssssst! He had no warning, just the dreadful, eye-watering, oily, disgusting spray from that black and white traveler. Mr. McAllister said it took him weeks to get rid of the smell. "I'm telling ya, Big One, it made me eye lashes curl right up. No one would come near me for weeks. My best friends even had the nerve to call me 'Mr. Stinks', can ya imagine that?"

It was clear, the tunnel needed lights. We had lots of Christmas tree lights in the garage, so I brought some of those over and they worked beautifully. After Miss Gloria plugged them into an outlet near the bushes, Mr. McAllister ran to the other end of the tunnel, hooking them to the side as he went. So far that has worked pretty well. I think it would be fun to go inside the tunnel myself, but I'd never fit. I guess I'll just have to be satisfied with the picture that Mr. McAllister drew for me.

When I arrived at Miss Gloria's house, I dragged the kayak down the hill and slid it into the creek. There was room for all of the stuff I brought and plenty of room left for the leprechauns. Some of them would probably want to go with Miss Gloria, so between the two boats everybody had a spot. As I was snapping the buckle on my life jacket, I heard the pitter-pat of bare feet and the muffled sounds of Irish accents. The gang was coming... and there were many of them! I counted as they slid out of the tunnel – 108, 109, 110, 111, 112.

The kids were dressed in their swimsuits, the adults were wearing their regular clothes, and all of them were wearing their life jackets. That's a lot of leprechauns to take on a picnic, but there were still quite a few back in the woods. Some didn't like the water, some stayed behind to help build an addition on the Day Care Den, and some just wanted a day to do nothing.

Miss Gloria joined us soon after, and we were ready to go. Eighty of them decided to go with me in the kayak, and the other 32 wanted to go with Miss Gloria. They were anxious to sit on the bow of the boat and feel the water splash up on them, and of course, Mr. McAllister wanted to be the captain on the voyage! "Do ya mind, Big One, if I go with Miss Gloria on this trip? She may be needin' my expert navigation advice, doncha know."

I told him it was fine with me. I had eighty others to keep me company. Anyone who went with me though, had to stay below. (The real story I think, was that the ones who wanted to join me in the kayak didn't want to get wet.)

We pushed off first and I began to paddle down the creek. If you've never seen a kayak, it looks like a canoe, except the only opening is an oval hole where the paddler sits. There is also a small hole in the front for storage. I was, of course, the paddler, and the 80 other passengers were somewhere inside the boat where my legs and feet were stretched out. I could feel them stumbling all over and occasionally one would trip over my legs and I'd hear, "Oh, don't mind me, Big One, just crossing over! No worries!"

Actually it tickled every time that happened, but things calmed down once we got going.

Some of the braver ones with me decided to open the small storage cover and sit up on the edge of it. From there they could see where we were going and wouldn't have to miss anything. It was a relaxing, sunny afternoon.

Well, if you must know, the 'relaxing' part didn't

last for long. All I can say is it's a good thing we all had life jackets on. A very good thing.

TOPSY TURVY

I heard the motor long before I saw the boat. Sound travels very quickly over water, and this sound got louder and louder by the second! It was obviously a motor boat coming, but usually the drivers know that the creek is a no wake zone, which means that you always have to go slow. Speeding in the creek and making huge waves, is against the law. I guess this hot dog teenager didn't know about that law, or maybe didn't care. Once we came around the bend I saw him coming towards us, and I knew we were in big trouble. I yelled down to the leprechauns to hold onto something and to tighten their life jackets. The words had barely left my mouth when the motor boat raced by us in a flash. Waves washed over the top of the kayak. We tipped from side to side, leprechauns flew out in all directions, and before I knew it, we had flipped upside down in the water. We were in real trouble.

I knew if I got out of the kayak, the leprechauns left inside would be in danger. Luckily we were in shallow water and I was able to push off the bottom with the paddle - right side up again. I yelled to the leprechauns below; they assured me that they were ok; I was so relieved! Those that had fallen out when we flipped, were also ok, and they were able to swim right over and climb back in. All I could think was thank goodness for the life jackets. That's when I realized that the ones who had been sitting around the edge of the storage cover were not there. "Where are Patrick, and John, and Alanah and Meghan? Oh my goodness- WHERE ARE THEY????" I screamed. They weren't down below. I couldn't see them anywhere.

Then, out of the corner of my eye I saw the lunches bobbing up and down in the water, and my turkey sub floating down the creek with Meghan and Alanah sitting on top of it. I yelled to them to grab a branch and wait on the shore for us. They were ok – but where were John and Patrick?

I searched and searched the water ahead of us and the water behind... nothing. My heart sank. Echoes of voices calling out for them rang from one side of the creek to the other. The air was dripping with fear. Quickly I paddled to the side, jumped out, and tied the kayak to a tree. We all walked along the water's edge to search for John and Patrick. In an instant our voices were drowned out by the sound of the motor... the boat was on its way back.

MISSING

The leprechauns scurried up the bank to avoid being washed away by the waves that were sure to come. I could see Meghan and Alanah about 75 feet down the creek, sitting safely on a rock waiting for us, so I knew they were safe.

The next few minutes were very scary as the boat screamed by, pounding the banks with hard waves. The driver laughed and waved as he passed; he only saw me, not the 76 others who were terrified and trembling, hiding from his carelessness.

Suddenly it hit me. Oh no! What if Miss Gloria had already set out in the rowboat? I wondered if she and the others were in trouble, too. I was sick with worry, but tried to think clearly. When the water had smoothed out again and the usual summertime sounds of the creek returned, I heard it. Then I heard it again.

"Well, whacha gonna do, leave us hangin' up here all day? We'd like some help getting our britches free, doncha know! Look up! We're up here!"

It was the most beautiful sound I think I had ever heard – John and Patrick's yelling.

"Oh my gosh... you're safe! You're ok! Hey everyone, they're here! They're ok!!!!!!!"

Way up, about 15 feet in the air, hanging from a branch of a willow tree, were Patrick and John. They were kicking their little legs, and waving their little arms and screaming at the top of their little lungs. We just hadn't heard them before because of the noise from the motor.

"Why didn't you use some magic to get down?" I yelled as I ran to the huge willow.

Patrick shouted back, "McAllister has told ya, hasn't he, that our magic fades when fear takes over. And I'm here to tell ya, fear took over, Big One! There's no magic to be found – not from this old man anyway. So please stop chattin' and get us down!"

Now I'm not very good at climbing trees, but luckily there was a huge rock under this one, and many low branches that made it easy for me to get to them. I carefully plucked John from his branch and sat him down until I could grab Patrick. Together, the three of us made it to the ground safely, into the waiting arms, and hugs, and cheers of the others.

"What about us?" came a shout from down the creek. Meghan and Alanah were still sitting on the rock, patiently awaiting their ride.

"We'll be right there. Hang on tight!" I called back. But before I could load all of the leprechauns back into the kayak and untie it from the tree, we heard the splashing of oars in the water. Miss Gloria and her crew were on the way to rescue the girls. Mr. McAllister stood on the bow, pointing to the spot where the girls sat.

We all cheered as they went by, Miss Gloria with her purple oars in the Silver Bullet, loaded with a bunch of leprechauns. Three cheers for Miss Gloria!

In no time, she pulled up alongside Meghan and Alanah, helped them in, and turned around to meet up with us again. There was another loud cheer, another round of hugs and lots of chatter. Miss Gloria and I just looked at each other and shook our heads. What an adventure it had been and the afternoon hadn't even started yet.

"Did you get swamped too?" I asked Miss Gloria.

"No, we were just about to leave the dock when I heard the motorboat coming, so I pulled the rowboat up onto the grass and we waited. I knew he'd have to turn around eventually because it gets too shallow just past our dock. Mr. McAllister was a good navigator and got us to you quickly. I'm so thankful you're all safe."

I gave her a very, very soggy hug. "Me, too," I whispered. "Me, too."

SLIDES AND RIDES

The whole terrible start left us wondering whether we should go back home and forget about the picnic, but we took a vote and decided to go to the park anyway. Why waste a beautiful day? The rest of the ride down the creek was uneventful, except for one thing. One pretty fabulous thing. Just before the last bend, we noticed flashing lights on the road ahead. There was no emergency, no accident, no problem. What it turned out to be was a teenager who was trying to be a hot dog in a motorboat, being stopped by the police. His boat was tied to a tree with yellow tape, and he was sitting in the back of the police car. I suppose they were having a nice conversation about being a responsible boater.

They drove off as we arrived at the park, and I

imagine his parents had quite a surprise when they saw their son come home in the back seat of a police car!

The park was crowded with lots and lots of families, but luckily they were all near the playground. That meant that we could easily get the leprechauns to the other side where there was one slide and a giant twirl around. The only bad part was we had to share it with a ton of geese. If you've ever gone to a park where there are geese, you know what the bad part is that I'm talking about! They can make a real mess.

We had lunch – not the lunch we planned, but a delicious one none the less. The sandwiches had floated down the creek, my turkey sub had sailed Meghan and Alanah to safety, and the rest had sunk to the bottom when we flipped. BUT, Miss Gloria had made a heap of fudge, a giant chocolate cake with sprinkles, and a load of Italian cookies. It was a delicious dessert lunch and no one complained a bit! Sweets, sweets and more sweets, and then it was time to rest and digest on the blankets before we tried out the slide.

As it turned out, the stairs on the slide were way too far apart for the leprechauns to climb, and their magic hadn't quite been recharged after the "incident", so we made an elevator out of the cookie container and some rope from the kayak. We put the container on the ground, attached it to the rope, threw the rope up around the rail at the top of the slide, and let the rest of the rope hang down. Five of them could step into the container and hold onto the side, while

Miss Gloria and I pulled the rope. Oh they screamed and whooped as they went higher and higher. Once they reached the top, they climbed out and took turns slipping down the hot shiny metal slide. Seems to me there were two Silver Bullets that day – a boat AND a slide! We had so much fun!

Oh yes, the twirl around was great, too, but we had to wait for lunch to really digest before we went on that. Spinning 'round and 'round is not a good idea when you've just eaten! Once they were ready to give it a try, the leprechauns held onto the metal bars and we pushed it faster and faster. It spun fast, so fast that a few little folks flew right off and landed in the puddle at the bottom of the water fountain! (That's because some of the leprechauns thought they were brave enough to hold on with only one hand. Foolish, but very funny.) Covered with muddy water and blobs of dirt, they sat there not knowing whether to laugh or cry. Eventually they decided to laugh, thank goodness, because it was hard for us not to laugh at the sight of them!

The best part of the day came when we went down to the edge of the creek where all of the geese were snacking. I was most grateful when I realized that they were gentle. Let me tell you, I have been chased by geese that were not so gentle; they had me running for my life, weaving in and out, screaming, as they nipped at my bottom with their beaks. Not fun!

But these geese were very sweet; maybe they had seen our ordeal earlier in the day and felt sorry for us. We fed them crumbs of left-over cake and they seemed to like that. And then an amazing thing happened. One by one, they swam up to the edge and nudged the little kids with their beaks. They didn't want to hurt them, they were letting us know that it was ok for them to climb onto their backs for a ride. We were a little hesitant to do that at first, but we put life jackets on the little ones and lifted them onto the soft feathered backs. Gently putting their arms around the long gray necks of the geese, the kids rode back and forth across the creek, as the sun set over the trees. It reminded me of the story *Make Way For Ducklings* with the swan boats in the Boston Public Garden.

By the time the geese had finished giving everyone a ride, the sky was painted with pinks and purples, and streaked with the golden rays of the sinking sun. It was time to go home. I'm happy to report that the trip home was perfect. Fireflies seemed to light the way along the creek. Crickets sang songs to welcome us back, and the moon turned on its brightest light as we walked back to the woods.

THANK YOU

Sitting around the fire at the meeting circle was a lovely way to end the day. We sang some songs, re-lived the frightening events of the afternoon, talked about how soft the goose feathers were, and cheered for Miss Gloria and her fearless rescue crew. It had been quite a day.

There was one point in the evening when Mr. McAllister walked away and was gone for quite a while. When he came back he was holding something behind his back. A hush fell over the woods, and the crackling fire was the only sound we heard. Miss Gloria looked at me as if to say, "What's going on?" but I had no answer for her, so I simply shrugged my shoulders.

Mr. McAllister made his way over to Miss Gloria.

In front of the flames of the fire, I could see the outline of an acorn in Mr. McAllister's hands.

He held it out to her."This is for you," he said as he twisted the acorn cap off. "It is filled with gold dust, too many pieces to count. Miss Gloria, we give you this tonight to say thank you for showing us what friendship looks like. You were a hero today and a true friend.

You will never be able to count how many pieces of gold dust are in here... think of that and know you will never be able to count our thanks for what you did today."

Miss Gloria didn't know what to say. "But I... it wasn't a big... I only..."

I leaned over and whispered, "Just say thank you. It was a big deal to them – and to me."

"Thank you," she said softly. "I am so proud to be your friend."

A cheer went up throughout the woods, because everyone knows a friend is a valuable gift indeed.

FRIENDSHIP

As I drove home that night I thought about all of the things that had happened not only that day, but in the years that have passed since I met Mr. McAllister. Life is full of interesting people - not one of them the same. I've met people older than I am, younger than I am, bigger, smaller, and WAY smaller than I am. I've met happy people, and sad ones, serious people and funny ones. Each time I meet someone new I hope to find something special about them, something that makes them shine. Miss Gloria and Mr. McAllister are good at shining. They are kind to each other and to all of the people they meet. They know that friendships are like flowers in a way; they grow if you take good care of them.

And so it is with Miss Gloria and Mr. McAllister,

they continue to take good care of each other. I just knew that's how it would turn out.

I still take my sketch book over with me when I go for a visit. I want to be prepared in case I see something so beautiful that I just have to draw it. I guess it's a way of catching a memory and keeping it safe until I want to see it again. And when that time comes, I open up the sketchbook and take a peek.

Hmmm... I wish I could draw friendship. But, maybe it's too big a thing to fit in a sketchbook.

THE END

ACKNOWLEDGEMENTS

I am so grateful for the thoughtful input of my mom, Jean Avery.

Cheryl Wilson and Tess Holloway, my lovely and forever supportive Southern Belles, thank you for the expert advice.

abundant thanks to Mak and Jess for their candid suggestions. Guess that's what magic feels like!

Many thanks to Mark Leiser for jumping into this project with boundless enthusiasm and a load of faith. I'm so proud and grateful to call you my friend. Your talent is truly MAGICAL!

an additional shout out to Mak for his naughty, nautical inspiration!

Sandy Barton is a retired elementary school teacher from Buffalo, New York. She has extensive experience in dealing with leprechauns and has had enough adventures with them to fill at least a hundred more books!

Sandy is the author of *Discovery in the Woods*, the story of how she met this charming little leprechaun, Mr. McAllister.

She is also the author of *Abjectedly Yours*, an adult memoir. It was co-written with Anthony Chandor, another dear, very unlikely friend, from Bath, England.

Visit SandyBarton.com for more information, or to contact her about author visits.

Mark Leiser is a part-time freelance illustrator, and full-time Parts Manager at Keyser Cadillac. He lives in North Tonawanda, New York with his wife and two daughters.

Mark is co-creator of *The Umbrella Man* and founding member of the Buffalo-based Fairfield Press. Learn more at FairfieldPress.com

Contact Mark at marklskwerl@yahoo.com

Thanks for reading Room For One More.

The magic continues…..

Made in the USA
Las Vegas, NV
06 March 2025

19156604R10069